D0378915

RESUME SPEED

LAWRENCE BLOCK

Subterranean Press 2016

First Print Edition

ISBN
978-1-59606-795-0

Subterranean Press
PO Box 190106
Burton, MI 48519

subterraneanpress.com

IN GALBRAITH, the Trailways bus station was a single room with a pitched ceiling, where a clerk dispensed hunting and fishing licenses and tobacco products in addition to bus tickets. There was no place to sit, so he waited outside, feeling exposed. As soon as his coach pulled up, he walked to the curb to board it, his bag in one hand, his ticket in the other. The bus was no more than a third full, and he found an empty pair of seats in the rear. He hoisted his bag into the overhead rack, dropped into the window seat, and let out a breath he hadn't even realized he'd been holding.

And then there was a small series of similar exhalations, of knots dissolving and tensions giving way. When the driver closed the doors and pulled away from the curb. When a sign announced the town line, and another said *Resume Speed*.

Minnie Pearl's home town, he thought. Years since he'd recalled the line. Years since he'd even thought of Minnie Pearl.

Another town, and another, and if they had *Resume Speed* signs of their own, he never noticed them. And, finally, the state line—and he drew a deep breath and let it out, and looked down at his hands, folded neatly in his lap.

Thoughts came, pointless thoughts, questions without answers. He blinked them away and breathed them away, and the bus stopped, and somebody got off and somebody got on, and the seat beside him remained empty, and the bus started up again. And, with or without a sign to prompt it, resumed speed.

His eyes closed. He slept.

━╸╱╽╲╺━

WHEN he opened his eyes he was in a town and the bus had stopped moving. Were they at a bus stop? No, they were idling at a traffic light, waiting for it to turn. He looked out the window, and two doors up the street was a diner. Neon spelled out its name: KALAMATA.

And there was a hand-lettered sign in the window. He squinted at it and couldn't swear what it said, but he had a fair idea.

And it felt like the right size town, big enough to have a traffic light, and far enough down the line from where he'd boarded. When they reached the station, he'd get off.

Unless they'd already stopped at whatever passed for a bus station in whatever town this was. He could have slept through it. Well, there'd be another town, and another diner. His ticket was good clear through to Spokane. If it stopped here he'd get off, and if it didn't he'd ride on, and either way it made no never mind.

Then the bus braked again, and he heard the driver say "Cross Creek," which was evidently the name of where they were. He'd never heard of Cross Creek, but it pretty much had to be in Montana, and on balance it made a more likely name for the town than Kalamata.

The seat next to his was still empty, so there was no one to disturb as he got to his feet and retrieved his carry-on from the overhead. When he reached the driver, the fellow told him they were just stopping to load and unload passengers. If he wanted a smoke break, he'd best wait until they got to Billings.

"I'm gonna leave you here," he told the man.

"Thought you was ticketed clear to Spokane."

"Somebody here I been meaning to see," he said. "Spokane can wait."

"Spokane ain't going nowhere," the driver agreed. "That all you got or do I need to open up the luggage?"

He shook his head. "Just this."

"Like the song." He must have looked puzzled. "You know. *Traveling Light*."

"Always," he said.

HE hadn't been counting the blocks, but he figured he couldn't be more than half a mile from the diner. A straight shot back the way he'd come. The bus hadn't turned off, just pulled up in front of the station—which happened to house a lunch counter of its own. He thought about stopping for something, maybe a grilled cheese sandwich, maybe a side of fries. But what kind of fool has a meal on his way to a restaurant?

Kalamata. Could be a Japanese tourist trying to say Calamity. He thought of Calamity Jane, who'd hung out a ways east of here, in Deadwood, if he remembered correctly. Pretty sure it was Deadwood. Although it could be that she'd gotten around some, which you'd have to expect from a woman with Calamity for a name.

His watch said 3:18, but maybe it was an hour earlier, maybe they'd crossed into a different time zone. So it was a little after three or a little after two, which amounted to the same thing in restaurant time. Past lunch and a ways to go until dinner, which made it down time, which was how he wanted it.

One foot in front of the other, and maybe it was a little more than half a mile, but it had to be there, and sure enough it was. KALAMATA, all in neon. And the hand-lettered sign, black block caps on a sheet of ruled paper torn from a spiral-bound notebook. EXPERIENCED / FRY COOK / WANTED.

He opened the door, walked in. Booths, tables, a counter along the wall on the right. Checkerboard tiles on the floor. Formica counter and table tops. Pennants on the wall—Cross Creek High, Montana State University. Two women sat over coffee at a booth in the back, smoke from their cigarettes drifting toward the ceiling. He'd smelled smoke in the air right away, against an overlay of cooking smells.

Pretty typical, really.

The Fry Cook sign was fastened to the inside of the door with clear tape, and he removed it, tape and all, and carried it to the man planted behind the counter. Stocky, jowly, black hair, thick moustache. Dark eyes that said they'd seen it all.

He handed the sign across the counter. "You can put this away," he said. "I'm your man."

The eyebrows went up a half inch. "Just get to town?"

"Does it show? Oh, this." He set his bag on a stool. "Just got off the bus."

"Where you worked?"

"Just about everywhere, one time or another. Some white-tablecloth joints, but mostly short order. I could give you references."

"What for? Work a counter and a griddle, a man can do it or he can't. Grab that apron off the hook there, then come on back and make me an omelet."

"What kind?"

"What kind you like?"

"For myself, I tend to keep it simple. Just cheese."

"You get a choice. Swiss, cheddar, feta."

"I like feta on a salad," he said, "but my first choice for an omelet is Swiss."

"So make a Swiss cheese omelet. We do three eggs, serve toast with it. White or whole wheat?"

"Whole wheat."

"And a side of fries."

"Got it," he said.

He got to work. He thought, feta cheese in the middle of Montana, and the guy looked like a Greek to begin with, so it wasn't a Japanese trying to say Calamity Jane, it was some kind of Greek word, and hadn't he heard it before?

Right.

HE put the omelet on a plate, added the fries, set it on the counter. He'd already buttered the two slices of toast and put them on a smaller plate.

"Why give it to me?"

"I thought you might want to taste it, see if it's okay."

"No eggs for me, no fried food either. Doctor's a pain in my ass. No, I don't need to taste it, I watched you make it, I know what it's gonna taste like. No, it's for you. Just off a bus, you gotta be hungry, unless you went and made a mistake and ate at the bus station."

"I didn't."

"Good, 'cause you'd be taking your life in your hands. Sit down, dig in. You want coffee? No, stay there, I'll get it for you."

He started eating, and forced himself not to wolf his food. This was breakfast and lunch, his first meal since an early dinner the previous evening, and he always liked his own cooking.

Halfway through, he paused for a moment and said, "Olives."

"How's that?"

"Kalamata," he said. "Rang a bell and I couldn't think what, but it's olives, isn't it? A fancy kind of olives."

The man smiled. "Big purple bastards. When I got 'em in stock, we put three in the Greek salad. Otherwise it's black olives from the Food Barn. It's not like anybody around here knows the difference. My father named the place, and it's not for the olives. It's a city in Greece, and he got the hell out as soon as he could. So you got to wonder why he stuck the name on the restaurant."

"You've never been there."

"And never will. If I was gonna fly somewhere, well, I wouldn't mind seeing Paris. But it'd be a miracle if I ever got out of Montana. It's not bad here, Cross Creek."

"It seems nice."

"And that leads to my question, which is will you stick around a while? Because you know what you're doing and I could for sure use you, but if you're just saving up for your next bus ticket, you know, it's not doing me much good if you take off just about the time you get the hang of how we do it here. You know what I'm saying?"

He nodded. "I'm not planning to go anywhere."

"All your life, you dreamed of making a home for yourself in Cross Creek, Montana."

"I never heard of it until I got off the bus," he said. "Anyway, I don't have any dreams."

"No?"

"Maybe once," he said, "but not in years. What I've learned, one place is as good as the next."

"You know that, you know plenty."

"I don't need much. A job where I get to eat my own cooking, a change of clothes, a place to sleep."

"You didn't get a room yet."

"No, not without having a job first."

"Well, you got a job. I been close to two months now since I let the last guy go. He was okay behind the stick, nothing special, but he missed too many days. And some mornings he came in with the shakes, and you knew right away what was making him miss those days. That a problem of yours?"

"No. But if it was, I'd probably say it wasn't."

"Yeah, soon as I asked I wondered why I bothered. You got a name?"

"Bill," he said. "Last name's Thompson."

"Good solid American name. Mine's Andy Page."

"Another solid American name."

"Well, I can say it's the name I was born with, but it wasn't Page until my father got off the boat. You're hired, Bill. Now let's figure out hours and money."

That didn't take long. They came quickly to terms and shook hands on it.

"So you got a job," Andy said. "You want another cup of coffee? Piece of pie? The pecan's real good."

"Not now, thanks."

"No, what you want is to get a room and settle in. There's a hotel a block the other side of the Trailways that's not too bad. Or there's a couple of places that rent rooms."

"I passed a place about two blocks back."

"Other side of Main? Big yellow house, got a hairdresser on the ground floor? That's Mrs. Minnick, and if she had a sign in the window, you want to get there before she takes it down. Her place is decent and she keeps it clean, and if you're a good tenant—

"I'm a good tenant."

"Yeah, I expect you are. Tell her you're my new fry cook. I think you'll like it there."

"I think I'll like it here."

"Well, I hope you do, Bill. I hope you do. Go ahead, get your room, get settled. Then come in tomorrow morning and you can start cooking some breakfasts."

THERE were things Andy had his own way of doing, but it was always like that, and it wasn't as though Bill Thompson was wedded to his own routine. He got the hang of it right away, and he remembered things. You didn't have to tell him twice.

And he was as much at home behind the counter as he was on the grill, and had a nice easy way with the customers. Not too easy, because an excess of familiarity could put people off. Especially the women, and Kalamata was a place where a woman by herself was comfortable sitting at the counter, and some of them liked to be flirted with and some didn't, and you needed to be able to size them up and read the signals they gave off. You didn't hit on them, that wasn't part of the deal under any circumstances, but some would think you were standoffish if you didn't flirt a little, and others would think you were overstepping boundaries if you did, and it wasn't a logic problem, you couldn't sit down and work it out with pencil and paper. You needed the right instincts, and he had them.

His room at Gerda Minnick's was as nice as any he could recall. Some years back he'd had a house of his own, a living room and kitchen in front, two bedrooms in back, on an eighth of an acre on the edge of town, and what town was it? He could picture the house, he could have drawn the floor plan, but he had to think to come up with Fort Smith, Arkansas. Little scrubby lawn, little spindly birch tree in the middle of it, and the bank that foreclosed on the house had been happy to rent it to him for less than he generally had to pay for a furnished room. The agent told him how the lease included an option to buy the property at the end of the year, and explained how it would be to his advantage to do so, and he considered it off and on. It was okay, it had to be a step up to have a whole house all to yourself, but the construction cut all the corners and the basement was damp, and what did a fry cook want with a home kitchen?

Moot point, as he'd left the city and the state with five months left to go on his lease.

At Mrs. Minnick's he had two flights of carpeted stairs to climb, and he shared the bathroom down the hall with another tenant, but the room itself was large and well-proportioned and the furniture was sound and serviceable and there were windows looking north and west.

There were rules. There was a TV in the parlor, but if he wanted to bring in a set of his own, he'd have to shut it off, or at least mute it, between the hours of eleven in the evening and 7:30 in the morning. No radio playing during those hours, either, and no loud music any time of the day or night. No running the shower between midnight and six. No guests, same sex or opposite, in the rooms. No smoking anywhere in the house. Spirits were not prohibited, but drunkenness was.

That was all fine with him.

She quoted him a price. "Or you could pay by the month for four times the weekly rate. That'll save you a few dollars every month, except in February it won't save you a nickel."

Was he supposed to laugh? He couldn't tell, she delivered the line in the same toneless tone that she'd told him when he could and couldn't take a shower. He thought of saying something about Leap Year and decided against it.

There was a week of April left. He handed over a week's rent, said he might switch to a monthly basis on the first of May.

He unpacked his bag, put his clothes in the dresser drawers. There was a lace doily on top of the dresser, positioned to cover the scar where someone's forbidden cigarette had burned itself out.

The only surprise to come out of his bag was his drinking glass, a cylindrical tumbler with six marks along the side to indicate volume from one to six ounces. He couldn't say when it had come into his possession. He hadn't bought it and he rather doubted anyone had, not as a drinking glass, because he rather thought it had started life as a jelly glass; whoever had used the last of the jelly had evidently decided the container was too useful to discard. And he'd evidently made much the same decision himself, finding room for it when he'd hastened to stuff a few things into his bag.

—•⁄∤∖•—

HE put the glass on the doily, then sat at the window until the sky began to darken. He walked down the hall, towel and dopp kit in hand, showered, shaved, made sure to leave the tub and the sink as spotless as he'd found them. He returned to his room, found a place for his shaving gear, propped his toothbrush in the six-ounce drinking glass, and hung the towel Mrs. Minnick provided on the bar where he'd found it, and picked out a T-shirt to sleep in.

When he'd filled his suitcase that morning, he'd fastened a money belt around his waist, underneath his clothes. He'd taken it off to shower, put it on again after he'd dried off. It held all his cash, except for a couple of hundred dollars in his wallet. Where to stash it? He looked around, decided it could wait until morning.

He got in bed, arranged the pillow the way he liked it. Closed his eyes, felt sleep moving in on him, took just the briefest moment to think about where he was. He'd done this before, he thought, and he could do it again. Hell, he was doing it again.

━ﾉ╿ヽ━

HIS life in Cross Creek became a life of regular habits. Six days a week, he worked a full shift at the diner, and the hardest part was figuring out what to do with himself on his days off. If the weather was good he might go for a long walk, might take in a movie. On rainy days there was no reason to leave the house, and barely reason to leave his room.

Once, maybe twice a week, after his shift at Kalamata was done, he'd stop in the downstairs sitting room and pass an hour in front of the television set. The two top-floor tenants were almost always there, one an elderly man who wore plaid shirts and got them buttoned wrong more often than not, the other a retired schoolteacher who always had a book with her to read during the commercials. Mrs. Minnick watched two shows every evening, the network news and *Jeopardy*, and disappeared for the night after the Final Jeopardy segment.

The tenant on his floor, whom he'd barely laid eyes on, never appeared in the TV room. She was morbidly obese and used two canes when she made her way to the bathroom and back. As far as he could tell, that was the only time she ever left her room.

He didn't need much in the way of diversion. The diner kept him busy from seven in the morning to seven at night. That was a long work week, but it wasn't all work, with fallow stretches between breakfast and lunch and again from mid-afternoon until five. And the work was work he was good at, work he enjoyed.

Anything he wanted to eat, he cooked it and ate it. Nothing wrong with that.

—✦—

HE stayed week-to-week at Mrs. Minnick's through May. On the last Thursday in the month, he finished his shift, walked home, and continued past his rooming house and down to the next block, where the sign was a braided rope coiled to spell out *The Stockman*. He went in, took in the familiar smell of a tavern, and walked up to the bar. He ordered a glass of beer and drank it, then looked over the bourbons and bought a pint of Old Crow. The bartender took his money and handed him the bottle in a brown paper sack.

He brought it home and stowed it, still in the sack, in a dresser drawer.

The following day he came straight home from work. He needed a shower, and took one, but decided Thursday's shave could last another day. Back in his room, he opened a window for the breeze and lay down on the bed for half an hour. He almost fell asleep, but didn't, and got up and dressed.

How, he wondered, did they come up with Old Crow as a name for a brand of whiskey? The label, with its illustration of a dapper black bird, held no clue. He decided that Crow, spelled that way or with an E at the end, was very likely the name of the original distiller.

Before uncapping the bottle, he took his toothbrush from the glass and found a place to set it down. He poured precisely two ounces of bourbon and seated himself by the open window. Someone was running a power mower, near enough so that he could smell the fresh-cut grass.

He took a moment to enjoy the smell, and then he raised the glass and breathed in the smell of the Old Crow, and enjoyed that, too.

Drank it right down. Liked the taste, liked the burn. It was smooth enough, but there was just enough of a burn to let you know that what you were drinking deserved a measure of respect.

Sat there, looking out the window, listening to the sound of the mower, breathing in the smell of fresh-mown grass.

After maybe five minutes he walked down the hall to the bathroom, where he rinsed and dried the glass. Back in his room, he put it back in its place, set the toothbrush in it. Returned the bottle to the dresser drawer.

—*/**—

THE following afternoon he came home, showered, shaved. Drank his two ounces of Old Crow. He had the same ration of whiskey each of the next two days, and on the first of June he paid Gerda Minnick four times the weekly rent.

"So you're month-to-month now," she said.

"It suits me."

She nodded thoughtfully, and came as close as she ever did to a smile. "Well, you're no trouble," she told him.

HE'D been wearing the money belt every day, though after a couple of days he'd begun removing it when he went to bed and donning it in the morning. The same night that he paid a month's rent all at once, he stowed the money belt at the back of the bottom drawer.

Partly, he supposed, because he'd seen no sign that anybody went in his room, except on the day when the girl came in to change the bed, leave a clean towel, and run the vacuum. He'd left little traps once or twice, just to see if she opened a drawer, and she hadn't done so.

So wearing the belt seemed an unnecessary precaution, and an increasingly cumbersome one, as the belt was thicker than it had been when he got off the bus. He wasn't earning a fortune working for Andy Page, but his rent—weekly or monthly—was low, and of course his meals were free. He'd bought himself a shirt and a second pair of shoes—he'd left with only the ones on his feet. Aside from that, he'd hardly spent any money at all.

For a couple of days it felt strange to be walking around without that pressure in the small of his back. But he got used to it.

THERE were magazines in the parlor, and he was leafing through a year-old copy of *Time* when he came across the card you mailed in for a subscription. It was offered with a guarantee; if you didn't like it, you wrote CANCEL across the invoice and mailed it back.

He filled out the card: William M. Thompson, 318 E. Main Street, Cross Creek MT. He didn't know the zip, but copied it from an address label on another of the magazines.

Mailed it in the morning and forgot about it.

Mail for tenants was stacked on a cherry end table in the vestibule. One evening there was a copy of *Time* on the table, addressed to him. He took it upstairs and turned the pages while he drank his two ounces of Old Crow, then set it on his own bedside table.

A few days later the bill came. He put it with the magazine, and over the next two weeks he received two more issues of *Time*, along with junk mail from another magazine—*Sports Illustrated*—and a few charities, including an organization that provided therapy dogs to wounded veterans.

When his next day off came around, he went to the Cross Creek Public Library. He'd stopped there before, but this time he applied for a library card, and for ID he showed his rent receipt, along with a copy of *Time* and several pieces of mail addressed to him. He thought he'd have to come back in a day or two for the card, but the librarian made it out on the spot.

"I never knew your name," she said, "but I recognize you well enough, Mr. Thompson."

"Oh?"

"From the restaurant. You wouldn't have noticed me, I always sit in a back booth, and I've generally got my face buried in a book."

"Next time," he said, "come sit at the counter."

He found a book to borrow, *Golden Spike*, about the building of the first transcontinental railroad. She checked him out and told him to bring it back for renewal if he didn't finish it in the allotted month. Otherwise there'd be a fine, and it wasn't steep, but why pay a fine if you didn't have to?

He went home, discarded the various pieces of junk mail he'd brought with him, and added his copy of *Time* to the stack in the parlor. He printed CANCEL on the *Time* invoice, mailed it back the following day.

The book was interesting. He'd thought it might be, hadn't just grabbed it off the shelf, but neither had he counted on getting caught up in it. For five nights running he sat down with the book and his two ounces of bourbon, just sipping the whiskey while he followed the story of the building of the Union Pacific Railroad, from the laying of the first rails in Omaha to the sinking of the titular golden spike at Promontory Summit, Utah.

The next day, a few minutes past noon, he was behind the counter at Kalamata when the librarian paused in the doorway. He flashed a welcoming smile, and pointed at a stool.

"Oh," she said. "I always want support for my back. But these stools have backs, don't they? I never noticed that before."

The special, he told her, was goulash. "My own recipe," he said, and she said that in that case she'd have to try it.

It was the diner's busy time, and he had meals to prepare and customers to serve, but they'd had a few exchanges by the time he took away her bowl and brought her coffee. When he set the cup in front of her she said, "Thank you, Mr. Thompson," and he told her to please call him Bill. That gave her the opportunity to tell him she was Carlene Weldon, and to please call her Carlene.

"Carlene," he said.

⌐╱▏╲⌐

THE next morning was Thursday, his day off. He rose and showered and shaved, although he'd shaved the day before, and left the house with *Golden Spike* under his arm. He'd stayed up late the previous night to finish it.

Carlene was at the front desk, talking on the phone. It gave him a moment to look at her without being himself observed.

Her hair was light brown, cropped close to her head, and in a large city on either coast she might have been taken for a lesbian. But he knew she wasn't.

Her face was heart-shaped, her features regular and unremarkable. Large eyes, a clear pale blue in color. She wore ironed jeans and a red-and-white checked blouse, and her body was neither slender nor plump. No ring on her finger, and no mark where one might recently have been. She looked like what she almost certainly was, a woman in her early thirties whose life offered everything a solitary life could provide.

Each of them, he thought, was just about the last thing the other needed. He was examining that thought, and wondering where it ought to lead, when she replaced the receiver and looked up at him. Her smile reached all the way to her eyes.

━╱╿╲━

"IF you liked *Golden Spike*—"

"I did, very much."

"Well, was it railroads generally? Or the history, the role the Union Pacific played in the development of the country? Because either way I could suggest a book or two you might like."

The answer came easily. "The history of it. I got a real sense of the way the country used to be, and the way people saw things."

She knew just the book. "It's set back east, and a number of years before anybody was thinking about transcontinental railroads." It was called *Wedding of the Waters*, and it was about the building of the Erie Canal. He opened the book at random, read a couple of paragraphs, and knew he wanted to read more.

He gave her his library card and she did the paperwork, then invited him to browse. Perhaps he'd find something else he liked. Oh, could he borrow more than one book at a time? She assured him he could. Up to five, she said.

He made a show of browsing, picking the occasional volume from the shelf, turning the pages, putting it back. He figured one book at a time was plenty, given that he'd paid his first visit to the library for the sole purpose of obtaining a library card.

Off to one side, an oak table held four desktop computers, with patrons seated at two of them. A sign explained that computer use was free, but there was a half-hour limit. You could print anything you downloaded, for a fee of 25¢ a page.

He stood there for a moment, then shook his head and turned away. Why spoil a nice day?

SHE was busy on her own computer when he returned to her desk, but she looked up at his approach. "I think I'll have my hands full with the Erie Canal," he said. "But I do have a question."

"Part of my job description, isn't it? Answering questions."

"What I haven't worked out yet," he said, "is where to eat when I have the day off. I could go back to Andy's, but—"

"But that way it doesn't feel like a day off."

"What it feels like," he said, "is I ought to put on an apron and wash up after myself. I figure one night a week it'd be nice to sit down someplace with a white tablecloth and let somebody wait on me."

She told him about three restaurants, only one of them in Cross Creek. She seemed particularly fond of the Conestoga Inn, located halfway between Cross Creek and Burnham, and he said it sounded really nice.

"But too far to walk to," he said.

"Oh, I'd say. It's twenty miles, or close to. You don't have a car?"

"Or even a license. Last place I lived you could get along fine without a car, and I went and junked the one I had when the transmission quit. My license was out-of-state, and I never bothered trying to renew it, or getting a new one."

She nodded, taking this in.

"What I'm thinking," he said, "is this Conestoga place sounds just right, except for two things. It's too far to walk, and it sounds like way too nice a place for a man to dine alone."

Something else for her to take in.

"So if you'd provide the transportation," he went on, "it'd be my pleasure to provide the dinner. As far as conversation's concerned, I figure that would be our joint responsibility."

━╱╲╲━

WHEN the waiter took their drink order, she asked for a Diet Coke. He said he'd have the same.

When he said something about her name, she said, "I'd have been Carl Jr. if I hadn't been a girl. And they were just positive I'd be a boy. There was this old Indian woman who supposedly always got it right."

"Until you came along."

"And I could have been Carla but my mother came up with Carlene instead. There's a singer, Carlene Carter, and there was a country song, a man singing about a girl from high school. *Carlene.* You would hear it a lot but you never hear it anymore. In thirty-four years I've never met another Carlene."

"Over the years," he said, "I've run into a fellow named Bill now and then."

"Well, I guess. Your full name's tons more common than my first name. Bill Thompson. Not quite John Smith, but not too far off."

"I could change it to Carlene, but people might look at me funny. Are your parents—?"

She shook her head. "He disappeared when I was in the second grade. We never heard from him, not a word. I couldn't guess where he'd be living, or even *if* he's living. And she died, oh, it's better than eight, close to nine years now. Nine years in November. Do you have any brothers or sisters?"

One of each, but he'd lost touch with both, and did either of them need to be in this conversation?

"No," he said.

"Neither do I. I used to think it would be nice, but they say the only child learns to be self-reliant."

"And are you?"

"Self-reliant?" She thought about it. "I guess so. I seem to be all right at getting along on my own. I got along when my father left and when my mother died, and when my marriage failed."

"You were married."

"I'm divorced longer than I was married. Two years married, three years divorced. That's a strange expression, isn't it? A marriage failing, like a business with too much money going out and not enough coming in. Except you couldn't explain it by bookkeeping. Have you been married?"

He shook his head. "Came close once or twice."

"What I came close to was backing out at the last minute. What the preacher says, if anyone has any objection to the wedding. You know, speak now or forever hold your peace? I was wishing somebody would speak up. My mama never liked him, but she'd have had to rise from the dead to make her objections known. There was really nobody to speak up, there was nobody at all but the minister and his wife and two witnesses who lived next door. I don't know why I'm going on like this, telling you way more than anybody'd want to hear."

"No, I'm interested."

"I'm in the house I grew up in. I never moved out, and when mama died it got to be my house, and he moved in, and two years later he moved out."

"And you're still there."

"And I'm still there. Born in Cross Creek and likely to die in Cross Creek, and sometimes that seems sad, all that road-not-taken business, and other times what it seems is fitting."

"Andy says he wouldn't mind going to Paris, and in the next breath he says he never will."

"Maybe everybody needs a place to never go to. For me it would be London. Did you ever read a book called *84, Charing Cross Road?* It's all letters, from a woman in New York to a bookstore owner in London. I forget what she was, a writer or an editor or something, but she could just as easily have been a librarian."

"And lived in Montana?"

"Anywhere. For twenty years they wrote each other letters, and all she wanted in the world was to go there and visit the store and meet this man, and by the time she finally went, the store was closed and he was dead."

"Another of those happy endings."

"Life's full of them. Anyway, London is the place I'll never go to. What's yours?"

Home, he thought.

What he said was, "Oh, I don't know. Maybe Hawaii."

THEY didn't talk on the ride home, but it was an easy silence, with no edge to it. She was a careful driver, her eyes on the road, and he passed the time watching her. He ran different lines through his mind, trying to find the right way to express a desire to see where she lived. He couldn't come up with anything that would seem natural. He could just say something, anything, about her house, and give her the opportunity to ask him if he'd like to see the place.

Wondered, sitting there and looking at her, if she was going through the same little dance in the privacy of her own mind. Wanting to invite him home, worried he might decline, worried he might accept.

She had picked him up a couple of hours ago in front of Mrs. Minnick's house, and now she braked to a stop in the same spot. He had the wild notion to invite her in, simply because it was against the rules. What he said was, "Well, this is where I get off."

"I had a really nice time, Bill."

"Did you? I know I did. Maybe we could—"

"Do this again? I'd like that."

"Do you ever go to the movies? I thought maybe dinner and a movie, one of these nights."

"I'd like that," she said, and rested her hand on top of his. Was it a good time to kiss her? Maybe, if they were standing on a doorstep, but not in the front seat of a Ford Escort.

HE passed the parlor without looking in and climbed the stairs to his room. He got ready for bed, then realized he hadn't had a drink. He could have had one before she picked him up, but didn't want it on his breath. Besides, he figured they'd each have one at the restaurant, but when she ordered a Diet Coke he'd followed her lead.

The hell with it, his teeth were brushed, he was already in bed. He turned off the light, drifted off.

THERE was another date, three nights later. He finished his shift, came home for a shower and shave, and this time he had a drink before she picked him up. They ate at one of the Cross Creek restaurants she'd mentioned, and the waitress greeted her by name.

"She was a year behind me in high school. Pregnant at graduation," Carlene explained, and frowned. "Like it matters, all these years later, but you never get over high school, do you?"

"I guess not."

She asked about his high school years, what they were like, and the truth was he couldn't remember them all that well. He said, honestly enough, that he supposed those were difficult years for everybody.

"Even when they're not," she said. "I read something, don't ask me where—"

"Probably the library."

"You think? What it said, there was a follow-up study on what the high school experience felt like ten years down the line. And the ordinary kids all said the same thing, how self-conscious they were, how isolated they felt, how they couldn't wait to get to the next stage in their lives. But you know what the cool kids said? The athletes, the class presidents, the beauty queens?"

"What?"

"Exactly the same thing! They looked to be having the time of their lives, and they were just as miserable as the rest of us."

The room was nicely appointed, with a high ceiling and plenty of room between the tables. Framed landscapes on the walls, suspended from the crown molding. But he felt they dished out better food at Andy's diner.

He wouldn't have said so, but she made the observation herself as they walked from the restaurant to the movie house. "They use fresh ingredients," he said, "and the presentation's nice. And it goes without saying that they're miles ahead in atmosphere. But whoever's doing the cooking has a few things to learn and a couple more to forget."

"Would you like to work in a place like that?"

"I've had a stint or two in fancier places. You know, upscale big city joints with a whole crew in the kitchen. I was way down in the pecking order, but even if I'd been higher up, I don't think I would have liked it. I'm happier behind the counter in a place like Kalamata, where nobody's likely to send back the wine because they don't like the way the cork smells."

"You can't get wine in Andy's, can you?"

"There you go," he said. "They can't send back what they can't order in the first place."

It was a weeknight, and the little theater was two-thirds empty. The film starred Jeff Bridges as a country singer who'd seen better days. There was a woman who thought she could save him, and he sat in his seat and saw himself and Carlene up there, playing out their parts.

Twenty minutes in, he reached over and took her hand.

He was still holding it when they rolled the final credits.

Outside, the air didn't feel like Montana. More like the Gulf Coast, humid and sultry. They walked toward her car, commented on the film they'd just seen, then fell silent. When they got to her car she turned to him and sighed and let her shoulders drop.

He said, "Before you drop me off, I'd love to see your house."

She turned, opened the door, got behind the wheel. Her house was on the edge of town, and neither of them spoke on the way there. She parked in the driveway, led him to the front door, unlocked it with a key.

Inside, he waited to embrace her until she'd closed the door. They stood kissing for a long time, and then she said, "Oh Jesus God," and took hold of his hand and led him to the bedroom at the rear of the house.

The double bed was made, with floral sheets and a tufted white bedspread. She drew the spread down, let it fall to the floor. Then she looked at him, her face slightly flushed, and took a breath, and pulled her dress over her head. She gave a moment to look at her, then stepped forward and turned so that he could unhook her bra.

WHEN she'd dozed off, he slipped out of the bed and got dressed. He had a hand on the doorknob when she said, "Wait."

"I'd better get on home," he said.

"You'll need a ride."

He said he didn't mind the walk. It would take him half an hour, she said, maybe more. And did he even know the route? She started to get up, but he put a hand on her shoulder and stopped her.

"I'll be fine," he said. "Get some sleep. I'll talk to you in the morning."

He hadn't been paying close attention on the ride to her house, but there weren't many turns and he'd always had a good sense of direction. He followed his instincts for ten or fifteen minutes, then came to a street he knew and had no trouble covering the remaining mile or so to Mrs. Minnick's house.

Spent the time recalling the warmth, the sweetness, the passion, the memories providing good company on the walk through the summer air, the sultry summer air.

The thought came to him that he could stay right here forever. And he wondered what he meant by that. Stay where? On these streets, walking back to his rooming house? In this town? With this woman?

Upstairs, in his bed, he wondered how long it would take to stuff everything he owned in the world into his carry-on. He'd bought a couple of things since he got off the Trailways coach. Would everything fit?

Funny thought to be thinking, at a time when he'd never felt so good. *Everything you ever wanted*, he thought. And was there anything on earth as dangerous as getting everything you ever wanted?

AS soon as the breakfast rush died down, he called her at the library. It was a brief conversation, but served to make it clear that neither of them regretted the previous night, and both looked forward to more of the same. He suggested dinner on the following night, and she said she'd pick him up.

He was waiting out front, and got in beside her when she braked to a stop. She asked where he'd like to go for dinner, and something stopped him from answering, and there was a moment when the silence stretched. But it was not an awkward silence.

At length she said, "Are you hungry?"

"Not really."

She waited for him to fasten his seat belt, then pulled away from the curb. Neither of them said anything for two or three blocks, and then what she said was, "The only thing I'm hungry for right now is your cock."

She was looking straight ahead when she said it, and she went on looking straight ahead, her eyes on the road, both hands on the wheel.

He reached to cover one of her hands with his.

"I said that out loud, didn't I?"

"Either that or I've started hearing things."

"It's not like me," she said, "to talk like that."

"Well, I'm no expert, but it seemed like a perfectly good sentence to me. Grammatically correct and all."

"'She was a slut, Your Honor, but she spoke proper English.' But, you know, it's the truth."

"That may be," he said. "Later on, though, you'll probably feel like a sandwich."

Her laughter was sudden, and rich. "Oh, that was just the right thing for you to say, Bill. It really and truly was. Bill?"

"What?"

"It's okay for me to be me, isn't it?"

IN bed the novelty hadn't worn off but the anxiety was gone, and he found her a bold and eager lover, giving and taking pleasure with gusto. Afterward, as he'd predicted, her appetite for food returned. She told him to stay where he was, and he closed his eyes for a moment and drifted off, waking up when she came back with two plates of scrambled egg and link sausages and bacon.

"Breakfast served at all hours," she announced. "Not as good as what you dish up every morning, I don't suppose."

He assured her the meal had nothing to apologize for.

They went back to bed, back to each other, and they talked idly while they pleasured one another. It had been such a long time, she told him, and he said it had been a long time for him, too. He answered her unspoken question by saying he hadn't been with anybody since he'd arrived in Montana.

"God, the responsibility," she said. "Representing my state. You know the motto?"

He didn't.

"'Oro y plata.' Isn't that wonderful? 'Gold and silver.' Well, that's what prompted them to settle the place, but still. It strikes me as pretty crass when the best thing you can think of to say about your state is what you can dig out of it. Bill? Am I any good at it?"

"Good at—"

"You know. I hardly did anything before I got married. And, you know, it wasn't much of a marriage."

After it ended, she told him, there'd been nothing for a while, and then a brief affair with a married man. She'd actually liked that he was married, because it limited their meetings to brief encounters once or twice a week, which was all she wanted from him. But he never got over feeling guilty about their affair, and when he told her one time too many that what they were doing was wrong, she agreed with him and told him they ought to end it.

"He was shocked," she said, "although he tried to hide it. He thought it was my job to ease his conscience. But I think he was probably relieved when it was over. I know I was."

Then there had been a salesman from Eugene, Oregon, who'd passed through, selling software to libraries. He took her to dinner and to bed, and she had a reasonably good time but never expected to see him again.

Nor did she, but a month or so later another fellow walked into the library and stopped at her desk. Not to sell software, or anything else, but to say Ed Carmichael had said he should stop by and give her his regards. She said that was nice, and he said it looked as though he was stuck in Cross Creek overnight, he'd just booked himself a motel room, and was there a decent place to eat in town? Say someplace where you could get a decent steak? And would she save him from having to dine alone?

She had dinner with him, and she had a couple of drinks, which she almost never did, and then she went back to his motel with him. Afterward he was enough of a gentleman to throw his clothes on and drive her back to the library, where she'd left her car. She drove home and spent more than the usual amount of time under the shower. She didn't feel dirty, not exactly, but she didn't feel entirely clean, either.

One week later somebody called her at the library. He was a friend of Ed's, or maybe he was a friend of Ed's friend, whose name she'd managed to forget. And he was in town, and Ed or Ed's friend had been talking about this fabulous steak dinner he'd had, but nobody could remember the name of the restaurant, and he wondered if maybe she was free that evening and—

"And I don't know what got into me, but what I said was his friend gave me the world's worst dose of gonorrhea, and if he really wanted I'd be more than happy to pass it on to him. And I'll never know what he would have said to that because I hung up on him."

"He's probably still trying to come up with a good line."

"All I knew," she said, "was I didn't want to be that girl. The one you call if you find yourself stuck in Cross Creek, Montana, and you buy her a steak and a couple of drinks, and you're home free. There may not be anything wrong with that girl, and she's probably having as good a time as the girl next door who collects Hummel figurines or the one down the block who rescues cats, but all the same I just knew she wasn't what I wanted to be."

"And here I am," he said, "stuck in Cross Creek, Montana."

"Here you are," she agreed, and laid a hand on him, as if to make sure of his presence. "First time I saw you, I thought, well, he'll wind up with the waitress."

"Who, Helen? I don't think—"

Helen was an aunt of Andy's who'd started waiting tables for something to do after her husband died. Carlene rolled her eyes, said, "I was thinking of the other one."

"I figured you meant Francie. Not my type, and you're just asking for trouble if you start up with a waitress."

"I think you're right. You're much better off with a librarian."

Besides, Francie was taken. He'd stood behind enough counters to know when a waitress was sleeping with the boss, and the first time he saw Andy and Francie make a point of not looking at each other, he'd put two and two together. He never said anything, or let on that he knew anything, and one night after he'd been at Kalamata a few months it was just him and Andy putting the diner to bed for the evening, and Andy felt like talking.

He almost said something now, to Carlene. Decided not to.

END of the week, Andy had an unusual expression on his face when he handed him his pay envelope. Not quite a smile, but close to it. He raised his own eyebrows, and Andy's smile widened.

"Better check it," he said. "Felt a little heavy to me."

He counted, and it was heavier by twenty-five dollars. He'd had a raise earlier, around the same time he started paying his rent by the month, and Andy had explained it as a sign of appreciation. It was, he assured him, no more than he deserved.

And now another raise. "Very generous," he told his boss. "Thank you."

"You've been good for the place, Bill. The goulash was your idea and your recipe. You rang it in as a daily special, and within a week we were getting requests for it, and now it's on the daily menu. People like it, and I can understand why."

"It's better now that we've got the right paprika."

"Maybe so, but there was nothing wrong with it in the first place. And the rhubarb pie. Not just thinking of it, but charming Mrs. Parkhill into trying her hand at it."

Hilda Parkhill was a rawboned widow who'd delivered two pies a day to the diner. One was always pecan and the other was usually apple.

"I just told her how much I missed my mother's rhubarb pie."

"Now she's selling us two pies one day and three the next, so it's good for her, and we're selling more pie than we used to, and you know what else? There's an interesting thing about the rhubarb pie, and I bet you know what it is."

"People usually order it à la mode."

"Like nine times out of ten. And if it doesn't occur to them, all it takes is a suggestion. 'You want a scoop of vanilla with that?' And they always do."

"Well, the rhubarb's tart, and the ice cream sets it off nicely."

"It's good from a food standpoint, and it's even better from a business standpoint. Can I ask you a question?"

"Go ahead."

"Did your mother really make rhubarb pie? I didn't think so. Bill, the raise is for the goulash and the rhubarb pie and all those scoops of vanilla, and if you keep on fattening up the population of Cross Creek, the next thing we'll do is open up a Weight Watchers chapter. Make money both ways, coming and going."

THE first time he spent the night at Carlene's was on a Wednesday. She'd always offer to drive him home, and more often than not he'd choose to walk, but sometimes the weather or his own tiredness would lead him to accept the ride. This time she pointed out that he didn't have to be anywhere in the morning, so why not stay? He said he'd been thinking that himself.

He heard her alarm clock but decided to give himself a few more minutes, and fell back asleep. It was almost ten when he woke a second time, and she was long gone. A note on the kitchen table said there was fresh coffee in the pot, and invited him to help himself to breakfast.

All he wanted was coffee, and he drank two cups of it, sitting at the kitchen table and feeling both at home and out of place. He pictured himself going through the rooms, opening dresser drawers, checking the closets. But he never left the kitchen, and when he'd emptied the coffee pot he took it apart and washed it, washed his cup.

He started walking home, then changed his mind and walked to the library. It was far enough from her house that she always took her car, and on the way he decided it was time to go ahead and get that Montana driver's license. He had a good job, he had a girlfriend, it was about time he got himself a car.

Her face lit up when he entered the library, and he liked that the sight of him could elicit that sort of response. She put a lid on it, greeting him as Mr. *Thompson*. He neared the desk, and she dropped her voice and said he was sleeping so nicely she couldn't bear to wake him.

He moved away to look for a book, then eased over to the computer station. Only one of the four units was taken, a young mother consulting a medical website, and he seated himself diagonally opposite her and hit a few keys. All he knew about the Internet was you used Google and went where it led you, and that's what he did.

He Googled 'William Jackson' and got a few million hits. He made the search more specific—'William Jackson + Galbraith North Dakota'. The first item that came up told him that Rear Admiral William Jackson Galbraith was born on 15 September 1906 in Knoxville, Tennessee, and he could have read on to find out how North Dakota entered into it, but that was already more than he needed to know about the man.

This was more complicated than he thought.

But he pressed on and got the hang of it. The two cities of size near Galbraith were Fargo and Grand Forks, and it was a bus from Fargo that had brought him from Galbraith to Cross Creek. Galbraith didn't have a daily paper, but both those cities did, and both papers had subscribers in Galbraith. Both papers had websites, too—for Christ's sake, even the Cross Creek Public Library had a website—and he checked to see what he could learn from the Grand Forks Herald and the Fargo Forum.

Not much. You could enter a search, but it wasn't like going to their office and looking through back issues of the newspaper.

He'd figured out the date, the day he got on the bus, and he entered that, but that didn't really get him anywhere. You'd think it would show him the newspaper for that day, but it didn't, and what it did show him was about as useful to him as the fact that Admiral W. J. Galbraith was born in 1906 in wherever it was. Nashville? No, Knoxville, and wasn't his life richer for knowing that?

It would be easier if he knew what the hell he was doing. But he had to figure it out for himself, because it wasn't something someone could help him with. *I want to know if anybody was murdered in Galbraith, North Dakota, on the 24th of April. I want to know if they know who did it, and if it's a guy named Jackson.*

No, better not.

'North Dakota Murders.'

That was better, better still when he added the year to the search term.

He scrolled through the entries, clicked on some and scanned them quickly, then returned to the list. Nothing in Galbraith, nothing about a man named William Jackson.

He thought about his last morning in Galbraith. Waking up suddenly, flung abruptly into consciousness. Sprawled facedown on his bed, still wearing all his clothes, even his shoes.

His shirt torn, ragged at the cuffs.

Scratches on his hands.

And ten or twelve hours gone. Some of them would have been passed in sleep, or whatever you wanted to call the unconscious state he'd been in. But the last thing he remembered—

The last thing was walking into a bar. He'd already been to two bars. First to Kelsey's, where he dropped in for a drink more days than not, and then to Blue Dog, where he went now and then, when Kelsey's failed to take the edge off. During all his time in Galbraith, he'd made no more than four or five visits to Blue Dog, and he'd never made it out of there without having a drink too many. Once he'd been asked to leave, but whatever he'd done couldn't have been too bad, because he'd been welcome enough on his next visit.

Each time, though, he'd had enough to earn him a hangover the next day, enough to poke Swiss cheese holes in his memory of the end of the evening—getting home, unlocking the door, taking his clothes off, putting himself to bed. He'd done all those things, and he remembered them, sort of. But the recollection was patchy, shifting its shape when he tried to bring it into focus.

But this last time his head was clear when he left Blue Dog. Nobody asked him to leave. It was his idea, and he never even considered going home. There was another bar on the next block, one he'd passed dozens of times without once crossing the threshold. It looked a little low-rent, he'd always thought. A little shady.

What the hell was its name? A woman's name. Maggie, Maggie's something or other.

Time he paid them a visit. He remembered running that phrase through his mind.

And what else did he remember?

Precious little. Opening the door, and the smell hitting him in the face. The smell was of a couple of kinds of smoke, wrapped up in spilled beer and shirts worn too many times between washings. It was a long way from being a pleasant smell, was in fact distinctly unpleasant, and yet there was something comforting about it. Embracing him, drawing him in. *You belong here,* it seemed to assure him. *Come right on in. You're home.*

The bartender was a tall blonde with a hard face. She was wearing a pink blouse, entirely unbuttoned in front, showing a lacy black bra.

Maggie's Turn—that was the name of the place. Was she Maggie? Maybe, but probably not. Maggie had probably lost the joint in a crap game, or sold up and gone prospecting in the Yukon, or turning tricks in Ybor City. If there ever was a Maggie. Maybe the bar's name was the title of a song, rock or country, it could be either one.

He didn't remember ordering a drink, but he must have, because he remembered her pouring it, remembered picking it up, remembered bringing it to his lips.

And remembered absolutely nothing after that until he came suddenly awake, like a radio switched on at full volume. Wide awake, still in his clothes, still wearing his shoes, and possessed with the certain knowledge that something had gone terribly wrong.

EXCEPT it looked as though nothing had. Nothing bad enough to make newspaper headlines, nothing to make William Jackson a wanted man.

His shirt has been torn, with a couple of buttons gone. That could easily be the result of a bar fight, and not necessarily much of a fight at that. A little pushing and shoving, a hand making a fist around the bunched-up fabric of his shirt, tugging enough to rip the fabric and send a button flying.

Scratches on his hands.

He'd looked at them and imagined those hands around a woman's throat. And her smaller hands, clawing at him, until the strength went out of them.

Not a memory, nothing of the sort. Just his imagination, taking in the evidence, fabricating an explanation for it.

But his hands showed scratches more often than not. He used them at work, he grabbed this and reached for that all day long, and he was forever picking up something too hot or scraping a hand against one thing or another. For all he knew the scratches on his wrists and the backs of his hands had been there before he went into Kelsey's, and thus long before he got to Maggie's Turn. He could walk around with scratches on his hands without ever taking notice of them.

Not until he woke up with jagged holes in his memory, and pure dread for what might have filled them.

But a few scratches didn't mean his skin was under somebody's fingernails. And how could he have choked someone to death without raising enough of a stir to register on the Internet?

Was there a way to clear his searches from the computer's history? He was fairly certain there was, but he couldn't figure it out, and decided it wasn't important. He logged out, stood up.

Time to get on with his life.

⌐╱╽╲⌐

THAT afternoon he filled out forms, showed his growing collection of ID, and applied for a Montana driver's license. The clerk established that he'd had an out-of-state

license and said if he could show it he wouldn't have to
take a road test. He explained that it had expired, and
long enough ago that he hadn't even held on to it. He
made an appointment for the road test.

There'd be a written test as well, and they gave him a
booklet so he could study for it. He glanced at the booklet
and saw that he could have taken the test on the spot,
and without reading the booklet. A sample question:
*True or false, in a three-lane highway the middle lane is used
for parking.*

He'd made his appointment for three in the afternoon, a dead time at Kalamata. You needed to show up
in a car for the road test, and somebody had to drive you
there because you didn't have a license yet. He didn't
want to ask Carlene to miss work, and Andy was out, as
at least one of them had to be there to flip burgers.

"You'll take my Toyota," Andy said. "Francie'll run
you there and bring you back. When we close tonight you
and me'll take it out for a spin, give you a chance to get
familiar with it. Every car's got things in a different place,
the lights and the wipers and all, and you don't want to
take a driving test with a car you never drove."

Andy sat beside him as he guided the car through the
streets of Cross Creek, then here and there on state and
county roads. "You won't have trouble," Andy assured
him. "It's like swimming, riding a bicycle. The memory

gets into your muscles and you can't forget. You could do it in your sleep."

"Some people do."

"Jesus, you think you're kidding," Andy said, and talked about a time when he'd fallen asleep at the wheel. "Drifted off the road, knocked down a road sign and clipped a telephone pole. Pretty much coasted into it, and it was a good thing I wasn't going fast, and an even better thing I pulled to the right instead of the left. It was a two-lane, runs north to Willard, and I could as easily have driven straight into oncoming traffic. So you never know, do you?"

When the time came, Andy tossed him the set of keys while Francie hung her apron on a peg. In the car she asked him was he nervous, and he said he wasn't. "I would be," she said. "You tell me something's a test, right away I'm all nerves. You got a car picked out, Bill?"

"Not yet."

"Andy's been talking about getting a pickup. You wanted, he'd give you a good price on this one."

He said it was something to think about. He pulled up at the building where he'd applied for the license, took the written test, and waited while a woman checked his answers and congratulated him on a perfect score. "Well, I was up all night studying," he said, and when she gave him a look he asked if anybody ever failed it.

"You'd be surprised," she said.

He returned to the car, and Francie drove him to the crossroads where they gave the road test. There were some folding chairs set up, and she sat and waited while a rail-thin man in a sort of generic khaki uniform had him drive here and there on back roads, going forward, backing up, making a three-point turn, and otherwise demonstrating that he knew the difference between an automobile and a sewing machine.

"Oh, hell, that's enough," the man said. "Most everybody passes, the average kid's done so much country driving by the time he gets here that he knows what to do. The ones from the Res, well, they don't need Montana's permission to drive on their own land, and when they want to be able to drive in the rest of the world, the only way they'll flunk the test is if they show up half in the bag. Which, I have to say, they sometimes do. You're okay, Mr. William M. Thompson. They call you Bill? Well, welcome to Montana's rolling highways, Bill."

SO just like that he had a car and a license. There was no reason he could think of not to buy the car from Andy, who told him he could have it at ten percent below the dealer buy price quoted in the Blue Book, and that he could pay for it in weekly deductions from his pay.

He could have paid cash for it, he'd gone on adding to the stash in the money belt, but he decided to split the difference, paying Andy half and arranging to have his pay docked for the rest.

"You've been saving your money," Andy said.

"Well, what am I gonna spend it on?"

"Not too much in Cross Creek. Of course you want to take your lady out for a nice meal now and then. Presents for Christmas and her birthday, and God help you if you forget Valentine's Day. Flowers or candy, and if you're smart it'll be flowers *and* candy."

Had he ever mentioned Carlene? Not that he could recall. Still, it was a pretty small town. It figured that everybody would know everything.

"I'll keep that in mind," he said.

"And while you're at it, thank God and the angels that you've only got one birthday to remember and one woman to send flowers to. Ah, don't get me started. Saving your money, Bill, that's a good thing. Time might come when you might want to make a little investment."

"Oh?"

"Never mind. We'll save that for another day."

THAT night he took Carlene to the Conestoga. She made more of a fuss over his car than it deserved, and he pointed out that it wasn't exactly a Cadillac.

"But it's a car," she said, "and it's yours, and that's exciting. When was the last time you owned a car?"

Back in April, he thought. He'd driven into Galbraith in an aging Buick, put a few bucks into transmission work while he was there, replaced two of the tires. And left it behind when he carried his suitcase to the Trailways station, because if they were looking for William Jackson the Buick would be something to key on.

When had he last owned a car? Well, technically, he probably still owned that Buick. It was a good bet they weren't looking for him, since he hadn't left a body behind in Galbraith, but he certainly wasn't going back for the car, and wondered idly who had it now. Wasn't a bad car, really. Burned oil, but you had to expect that.

What he said was, "Oh, it's been a while."

He'd picked her up at the library, and stopped there so that she could get her car, then followed her back to her place. He wasn't really in the mood and would have just as soon gone on home himself, but he didn't think that would go down too well.

And he wound up in the mood soon enough. "There's something I read about," she said, avoiding his eyes, and

went on to do things that suggested a fruitful apprentice-
ship in a bordello in Port Said.

⁓⁄⁀⁀⁓

HE drove to Kalamata. There were four parking places
behind the diner, and Andy, who walked to and from
work, had kept the Toyota in one of them for as long as
he'd owned it. "The spot goes with the car," he'd said.
"You get all the comforts of home with Mrs. Minnick, but
what you don't get is a place to park."

He left the car in his spot, walked home, then remembered he was just about due for another bottle of Old
Crow. At two ounces a day, a pint was gone in eight days.
Lately he'd begun to buy fifths instead, and a fifth was
twenty-six ounces and change, so it lasted him that much
longer. But there was just one drink left in the bottle, and
a little less than a full drink at that, so he kept on until he
was standing at the bar of the Stockman.

Without asking, the bartender reached for a fifth of
Old Crow, then paused before slipping it into a paper
sack. "Got a special on J. W. Dant," he said. "Generally
more expensive than Crow by a dollar a bottle, and somebody decided that this month it's three dollars cheaper."

While he thought about it, the bartender set up a
shot glass and filled it from a J. W. Dant bottle. "On the

house," he announced, "so you can make an informed decision."

He picked it up, drank it down. "Tastes the same as the Old Crow."

"All you miss out on," the bartender said, "is that slick-looking bird on the label."

He nodded, and the man put the Old Crow back on the shelf and slipped the Dant into the paper sack.

He paid for the bottle, reached for his change, then stopped himself. He ordered another shot of the Dant, and stood there looking at it for a long moment before he picked it up and drank it down. Then he ordered another.

And that, he decided, was enough. He'd had enough to feel it, and he did feel it, and it wasn't a bad feeling. But it was as good as he needed to feel, and as much as he needed to drink, and he walked home carefully, used his key carefully, climbed the stairs carefully.

He put the bottle away, and now he had two bottles in the drawer, and that wouldn't do. There was less than a full drink in the Old Crow bottle, and it occurred to him that he probably ought to finish it now, so that he could get rid of the empty bottle on the morning.

Decided it could wait. Decided the dresser's bottom drawer, which no one but he himself ever opened, could hold two whiskey bottles for another day or two, and was better equipped to do so than he was to hold another slug of bourbon.

But there was something else to tend to before he got into bed.

He fetched his money belt, went through the bills and found his North Dakota driver's license. It bore his photograph, along with the name of William M. Jackson. He pulled out his new Montana license and compared the two pictures, and decided that they looked more like each other than either of them looked like him.

He'd retained the North Dakota license in case he ever needed it for an emergency. If he'd had to drive, it was at least a valid license, with a couple of years to go before it would expire.

You couldn't tear it up, it was some sort of laminate of plastic and cardboard, and while it would probably burn, it might raise a stink in the process. He spent twenty minutes using his Swiss army knife's scissors to cut the thing into tiny fragments. The license resisted cutting, and it was hard to get leverage on the little scissors, and by the time the job was done to his satisfaction, he felt as sober as he'd been when he first walked into the Stockman.

In the bathroom, before he readied himself for bed, he flushed away the innumerable shreds of his old license. In bed, during the few minutes he waited for sleep to come, he thought that he had everything a man could need.

He had a job and a place to live, he had a girlfriend who was good company in and out of bed, he had a car and a place to park it and Montana's official permission to drive it wherever he wished.

Everything a man could need.

━━╱╿╲━━

HE woke up with a headache and a dry mouth. But his memory was crystal clear. He wondered at some of what he recalled. Why had a quick stop to pick up a bottle of whiskey turned into three drinks in quick succession?

No answer to that, but no harm, either. Two glasses of water got rid of his thirst, and as many aspirin did the same for his headache.

Checked himself in the mirror, saw the same face he always saw. No better, no worse.

Off to greet the day.

━━╱╿╲━━

A week later he worked the breakfast shift by himself, and Andy came in at lunchtime. When the noon rush faded, Andy said, "You know something, Bill, you got me thinking."

"Oh?"

"About pie. About pecan pie, specifically."

"There's a piece or two left, if you want one."

"How you got me started," Andy said, "is rhubarb pie and vanilla ice cream. Every time I sell a piece of pie, I ask, 'How about a scoop of vanilla ice cream with that?' And with rhubarb the answer is usually yes, and with the other pies it's sometimes yes and sometimes no. It's yes enough of the time to make it worth asking, but it's not the same as with the rhubarb."

"Well, there's a natural affinity, I guess."

"Affinity. I guess there is, and that's where I'm going with this. I'm thinking I'll start carrying a new flavor of ice cream, and can you guess what it is? Butter pecan."

"For the pecan pie."

"You don't think that rings the bell for affinity?"

"I'm just trying to figure how they'd taste together," he said. "Not bad, would be my guess, but what bothers me is the sound."

"The sound?"

"Pecan and butter pecan," he said.

Andy considered, nodded. "Like an echo."

"Well, sort of. Like a double dose of the same flavor, but there's no question you're on to something. Rhubarb and vanilla, pecan and what?" He'd known right away, but took his time coming up with it. "Oh," he said, "I bet that would work."

"What's that?"

"It's just an idea, but I'm thinking rum raisin."

"'One pecan pie coming up, and how about a scoop of rum raisin with that?' Oh, I like that. I can just about taste it. You ever try it yourself?"

"I haven't got much of a sweet tooth, Andy."

"No, come to think of it, I don't recall ever seeing you eating pie *or* ice cream. But you're a genius at knowing what goes with what. You know what else I like about it? They're already feeling pretty daring ordering a rich dessert, and now they get to top it off with something that sounds like drinking. You happen to know if there's any actual rum in rum raisin?"

"It's probably just rum flavoring, wouldn't you think?"

"Well, I don't suppose you need a liquor license to sell it. It's just that there'll be some of them who'll have to know. There's these four women come in every Wednesday after they work on their quilts over at the First Methodist. You know the ones I mean?"

He nodded. "Always take a booth."

"And generally the same booth every time, and when I remember I save it for 'em. 'Now one of you young ladies better have vanilla, and be the designated driver.'"

"You've got your lines all worked out."

"What I'll do, I'll call in an order right now before I forget. Rum raisin ice cream. Have to wonder how the

Mormons feel about it, and I guess we'll find out, won't we? Oh, we're gonna have some fun, Bill. And you know what else? We're gonna sell us some ice cream."

LATER that week he drove to Carlene's to pick her up, and she motioned him inside. As soon as he crossed the threshold his nostrils filled with cooking smells and he knew they weren't going anywhere.

She'd set the table with proper china and cloth napkins, and she made him sit while she filled two plates in the kitchen and brought them to the table.

It was a Belgian-style beef stew, with the cubes of beef cooked in beer, along with potatoes and root vegetables. She'd done the prep work the night before, then switched on the slow cooker before she left for work.

"It's very frightening," she said, "to prepare an elaborate meal for a man who cooks for a living. But it's good, isn't it?"

It was delicious, and he told her so. She'd bought three bottles of the beer, a dark German brew, and only used one in the stew, and they each drank a beer with the meal. Later they shared the sofa and watched TV and wound up in bed. Their lovemaking was slow and gentle, and then passion took hold of both of them.

Afterward he caught himself dozing off, and started to get up. She said, "Don't, you're tired."

"They'll see my car."

"So? It's a perfectly nice car. It's nothing to be ashamed of."

"I meant—"

"I know what you meant, and do you really think we're likely to shock anybody? Everybody knows we're an item."

"An item."

"We can decide what to call it in the morning."

And in the morning, without raising the subject of what to call whatever they had, she suggested he might want to keep a change of clothes at her house. And, oh, a spare razor. That sort of thing.

He had a shower, put his clothes back on. Drank a cup of coffee.

IT had been six weeks since he bought Andy's Toyota, and he'd been wondering when they'd have that conversation about an investment he might want to consider. He was in no rush, but he knew it was coming.

Cross Creek got snow flurries one evening, and then two days later the first snow of the season fell overnight and melted in the morning sunlight. That gave the breakfast crowd a topic of conversation, and everybody had something to say about it, none of it very interesting.

When the room had mostly cleared, Andy drew two mugs of coffee and gave a nod to Helen, who took it as signal to take his place behind the counter. "Come on," he said to Bill. "Want to talk with you."

When they were seated across from each other in a back booth, he said, "Conversation I been having with you in my head for months now, and it's time I came out and let you know what I've been thinking. Though you can probably guess."

"Just so you're not about to fire me."

"Yeah, building up my courage." He sipped his coffee. "The hell, you have to know where this is going. I been running this place all my life, it feels like, and I'm not getting any younger, and if there's anything I want to do in my life, it's getting to be time to do it."

"Like that trip to Paris."

"Which is never gonna happen, except it might, except how could it if I'm running this joint? You see where this is going."

"I guess I do."

"What keeps me here is what am I gonna do, lock the doors and drop the keys in the storm drain? I suppose I could do just that. This town's been good to me, and same for the people who eat here and the ones who work here, but that doesn't mean I owe anybody anything but a fair wage or a good meal. And if Kalamata closes, who's gonna go hungry?"

Andy was looking off to one side, looking at nothing but the past and the future. Looking for words, Bill thought, and gave him time to find them.

"You spend your life running a joint, do you want to walk away from it? Well, you do and you don't. You want to leave it in good hands."

Silence again, and his turn to break it. "I have a feeling you're not talking about Helen or Francine."

"It's a good business, Bill. It's fed me and mine for a lot of years, and put clothes on our backs, and I have to say it's as recession-proof as a funeral home. People gotta eat. They may cut back on the high-ticket joints, but they'll still show up for their eggs over easy." His face softened. "And their goulash," he said. "And their rhubarb pie."

"With a scoop of vanilla," he said. "Andy, you said it yourself, it's a good business. Which means it's worth money, which means you can't give it away."

"No, I'd need to sell it."

"And that's only right, and if I had the money—"

"Could you get your hands on twenty-five hundred dollars?"

He had a little over twice that in the money belt.

"Say I could. What would that buy me? The coffee urns and a couple of counter stools? Jesus, besides the building you own the structure, the real estate."

Andy held up a hand to stop him. "I been talking to my accountant," he said, "and it works. You'll pay me out of your receipts. Twenty-five hundred down and the rest according to a formula. I forget how many years you'll be paying me off, but in the meantime you'll be making a decent living, and at the end of the rainbow it's all yours, free and clear."

"Jesus," he said.

"Now what you want to do is think about it, Bill. It's not like I want to go home and start packing. I figure I want one more Montana winter so I don't forget what they're like, so we got plenty of time for you to decide and for the accountant to work out the details and the lawyer to put the paperwork together. But what I'd love to do is shake your hand sometime in May or June, and once that's done, you're the owner and proprietor of Kalamata."

"It's a lot to think about."

"Of course it is—or it's a no-brainer, depending how you look at it. Incidentally, Kalamata. No reason you can't change the name to something you like."

"What would I change it to?"

"Well, half the town calls it the Calamity. You could change the sign and make it official."

"What everybody calls it," he said, "is Andy's."

"And they'll keep on calling it that for the first year or two, and then it'll be Bill's, and pretty soon not one person in ten'll remember it was ever anything else. Jesus, I'm getting choked up, and it's a fucking diner is all it is. A diner I'll be glad to walk away from, and the day you cooked that first omelet, what came into my head is maybe this is the guy who'll take the place off my hands. So you think about it, okay?"

HE thought about it off and on for three days. Then he told Carlene.

They were on her couch eating pizza in front of her TV, and she just listened while he recounted Andy Page's offer. She was very good at listening, at giving a person room to talk, and that was one of the things he particularly appreciated about her.

When he finished, she remained silent for a moment, and then what she said surprised him. She asked him if he'd change the name.

"I don't know," he said. "Do you think I should?"

"I guess that depends on how much you'd change the place itself."

"How?"

"I don't know. Would you redecorate? Redo the menu?"

"It wouldn't hurt to throw a coat of paint on the walls, but there's no rush, and it won't look that different afterward, just a little less shopworn. The menu, well, I've been making changes now and then, and I'd keep tweaking it, you know? I could take a couple of the Greek dishes off the menu. Pastitsio, most customers don't know what it is. Change it up and call it lasagna and I bet it'd move faster."

He told her some more of his ideas. She said, "You're excited about it."

"A little."

"And something else. What's holding you back?"

"Well, what do I know about running a restaurant?"

"A lot, I'd say."

"About cooking, and selling food. What do I know about being a boss?"

"You've watched Andy."

And a lot of other men over a lot of years. "You can only learn so much by watching," he said. "Hiring and firing, dealing with suppliers. It could be a headache."

"I guess it could."

"He was going nuts before I showed up. I could run the place the way he did, with just Francie and Helen, but I'd be working myself to death unless I found somebody."

"You'd put a sign in the window," she said, "and some handsome stranger would take one look at it and hop off the bus."

"Yeah, there you go. And I'd have to hope he spotted some equivalent of a hot librarian and decided to stick around. Andy makes decent money, but that's no guarantee that I would. I could go broke."

"And if you did?"

"I'd give the place back to him and get on the next bus."

"Or you could give the place back to him," she said, "and not get on the bus. But first you'd have to go broke, and I don't think that would happen. You're too good at what you do."

And a little later he said, "You know, maybe I'll hit the library tomorrow. Check out something on restaurant management."

HE showed up mid-morning, browsed the business section and the food section, carried a couple of books over to a table, sat down and read. At one point he realized nothing he read was registering. The words just passed in front of his eyes and trailed off into the distance.

He re-shelved the books. You were supposed to leave them, on the premise that you couldn't be trusted to put them back in the right place, but he remembered where they'd come from and managed to put them where they belonged.

Went over to the computers. All four were unattended, and he sat down all by himself and logged on, did a little idle surfing. Checked out a few recipes for lasagna, which seemed to be a dish with infinite variations and no ironclad requirement beside big flat noodles, and for all he knew even that was negotiable.

Could be interesting. Try different recipes, find the one he liked the best, then play with the proportions and the seasoning until it was just the way he wanted it.

Other dishes he could experiment with as well, menu staples he'd learned to make the way Andy made them, but if it was his diner he could make his own rules.

Thought about William Jackson and Galbraith, North Dakota. But nothing had happened, he reminded himself. He'd left town, had felt the hot breath of the hound of hell on his neck even as the bus took him away from there, but it was all unnecessary, wasn't it?

If he thought about it clinically, it was just a fear, one that came to him automatically when drink left him with holes in his memory. If there was a span of time unaccounted for, he could only imagine the worst. He must have done something wrong, something unspeakable.

Otherwise why would his memory insist on blocking it out?

And so he'd feared the worst, and acted accordingly. Pure unreasoning fear, based on nothing.

He drew a breath, held it for a moment.

And then he did something he hadn't done in longer than he could remember. Not since he got to Cross Creek, not once in Galbraith, nor in the town before Galbraith, or the one before that.

He called up Google, keyed "Walter Hradcany" into the search box. Hit *Enter.*

And the entries popped up, even after all the years. There were a slew of them, mostly in West Texas, but some more recent ones popped up on websites devoted to unsolved crimes. The stories they told differed in details, but not in their essentials. A young woman named Pamilla Thurston had been found strangled to death in the house trailer she had previously shared with her estranged husband. She'd been dead for 48 to 72 hours before her body was found.

Inevitably, suspicion centered upon the husband, but he held up under questioning, and so did his alibi. Pamilla had last been seen at a roadhouse just outside the town limits of Plainview, no more than two miles from her residence. She had been a regular patron, especially since her husband had moved out, and left with one man or another more often than not.

It was hard to determine which night had been her last, and hard for anyone to recall with certainty who'd been her companion on either of the possible final nights. Several names came up, and several men had the challenging task of proving that they hadn't gone home with Pamilla. But one man whose name came up was a short-order cook named Walter Hradcany. No one remembered seeing him leave the roadhouse with Pamilla, but two people recalled he'd been talking with her, so the Hale County cops went looking for him.

And found out he'd disappeared. One day he was there in Plainview and the next day he was gone. He was supposed to work the early shift at Grider's Family Restaurant, but he never showed and never called in. He'd been one of the permanent guests at a budget motel, paying by the week, and he'd left clothes in the dresser and toilet articles in the bathroom, and his car was still parked in front of his unit. It seemed possible that he was dead himself, murdered by the same person who'd killed Pamilla. Or he might have died by his own hand, wandered off into the middle of somebody's wheat field and shot himself.

His body never turned up. And the DNA they got from the hairs in his comb matched what they found under Pamilla's fingernails. So as far as local law enforcement was concerned, Walter Hradcany was more than a person of interest. They had enough on him to close the case, but they couldn't clear it, because they never turned up a trace of him.

A distinctive name, Walter Hradcany.

There had to be a way to clear the computer's history, and he looked for it until he found it. He erased everything for the past two days, and then he built up a little fresh history, searching once more for recipes and restaurant management tips.

Not that the Walter Hradcany search could be entirely expunged. He'd seen enough TV to know that anything you did on a computer left a spoor that lingered forever. On the hard drive, in Google's infinite files, or in some metadata base in Washington.

But they'd have to be looking hard to find it, and they'd need a reason, and they didn't have one. And he didn't intend to give them one, either.

—✦—

THE next day he opened up at Kalamata and served a lot of breakfasts. Around eleven he almost said something to Andy, but he let it go until the middle of the afternoon.

Then he said, "Well, I thought it over, and I could just as easy have answered you on the spot. It's a wonderful offer and I'd have to be crazy to say no to it. Only bad thing about it is I'll miss working alongside of you."

"And the only problem you'll have is finding a fry cook as good as the one I found. I'll get my guy to put something on paper, but that's just the formalities. Far as I'm concerned, we got ourselves a deal."

HE spent the rest of his shift thinking of the computer search, thinking about Plainview, Texas. Out in the Panhandle, and the name fit; the only view you had out there was a view of the Plains.

Nice enough town.

Pamilla Thurston. He'd never known her last name, or the unusual way she spelled her first name. Still didn't have a clue how she'd pronounced it, same as if it was Pamela or to rhyme, sort of, with vanilla.

Pam, that's what people called her.

He couldn't really remember what she looked like. When he tried to picture her, the image that came to him was a blend of photographs he'd seen in the newspaper.

So what did he remember?

Talking to her, buying her a drink. He'd been wearing a string tie—well, it was West Texas, it was a cowboy bar. And she'd stepped in close and snugged up the turquoise slide, letting her body lean a little against his, giving him a nose full of her perfume.

That was all he remembered.

Until he woke up in his motel room, all his clothes on, including his boots. Sprawled on the bed, his feet trailing on the floor.

Nothing in his memory after she'd tightened his tie. Nothing in his head but the sure knowledge that something bad had happened.

He was on a northbound bus, and halfway to Lubbock he started to wonder if he'd lost his mind. Wake up with a bad feeling and skip town like a shot? Leave everything behind, even the car that would have been a lot more comfortable than the damn bus? All that because he was hungover bad enough to think something must have happened?

That was a few minutes before he was aware of the soreness in his forearms. Noticed the blood that had seeped through his shirtsleeves. Rolled up the sleeves, saw the scratches.

IT wasn't until the following evening that he saw Carlene. He'd expected to tell her of his decision, but somehow kept letting the opportunity go by. They went to a movie, and his mind kept wandering from the story, rehearsing a conversation in his head. Then, by the time the film was over, he'd decided to let it ride.

But he didn't want her to hear it from someone else first, and news got around in Cross Creek. A day or two later he was looking for a way to ease into the subject, when she made it easy for him by asking if he'd decided yet.

"I think I probably decided the minute Andy popped the question," he said. "He called it a no-brainer, and he was right."

"Still, it's a big step. I'd say you were wise to take time to think it over. Well, congratulations, Mr. Restauranteur."

"Right. Next thing you know they'll give me a TV show, like what's his name."

"Emeril?"

"I was thinking of that guy who goes around the world eating bugs and worms."

"Anthony Bourdain. We've got several of his books in the library."

"Well, if I ever need to know how to cook a cockroach…"

"You'll know where to look. Honey, we should celebrate. This time I'll take you out to dinner. Tomorrow night?"

"Sure," he said. "That'd be great."

Their lovemaking was practiced but intense, and even as he took his pleasure he felt a wave of sadness roll in on him.

When her breathing slowed, he slipped out of bed and put his clothes on. He drove home, left his car in his spot at the diner, and walked on home.

THE following evening he called her from Kalamata. He was feeling under the weather, he told her, and there was fresh snow on the ground with more of it in the forecast, and tomorrow or the next day would be a better choice for their festive dinner. He'd fix himself something before he left, then go home and make it an early night.

"Feel better," she told him.

There was a piece of pecan pie left, and he decided that would do him for dinner. He topped it with a scoop of rum raisin ice cream. It had turned out to be a successful combination, and had in fact upped the sales of both components, the pie and the ice cream.

And he could see why. They were a good match, the rum raisin and the pecan.

He could make the place work. Hell, it worked already, and his mind kept coming up with ways to make it better.

HE walked home. There was snow on the ground, but the sidewalks were mostly cleared, and his shoes could handle a few inches of snow with no trouble. He let himself into Mrs. Minnick's house, stomped his shoes clean in the entryway, went up to his room. His coat was a heavy-duty Buffalo plaid from Walmart, all wool, all red and black squares, and once he'd hung it on a doorknob he retrieved the bottle of J. W. Dant from the bottom drawer.

It was a little more than a third full. He poured two ounces of whiskey into his drinking glass and moved his chair over to the window. It was peaceful, with a little snow on the ground, and of course it was quiet.

It suited him here, he thought. He'd slept well in this bed, in this room. It was so remarkably convenient to Kalamata that even now, when he owned a car, he never used it to get to and from work. The walk each morning got the blood moving in his veins and set him up for a day's work. The walk home each night gave him a chance to shed all the workday tension on the way.

Would he be able to stay?

Because it was perfectly appropriate for a new man in town, a fry cook, a counterman, to live in a furnished room. But he was no longer a new man in town, no longer a drifter who'd got off a bus and grabbed a job to support him while he figured out where to go next. He'd been there long enough for Cross Creek to know who he was, or at least who they thought him to be. He was Bill, worked alongside Andy at Kalamata, and maybe he ought to occupy living quarters that suited his station in life.

Not that there was anything less than respectable about Mrs. Minnick's.

Soon everybody would know he'd arranged to take over the diner. And not long after that he'd be its owner, and did a man who owned a restaurant live in a furnished room, however respectable it might be?

A man in that position ought to have an apartment. Ought to have a house, really.

He lifted the glass, found he'd drained it. He considered the fact, and then he walked to the dresser, where the bottle stood waiting. He'd left it standing on top of the dresser instead of returning it to the drawer, perhaps in anticipation of this moment.

He poured another two-ounce measure of bourbon into his glass and returned to the chair. He took the glass of whiskey with him, of course, and this time he took the bottle, too.

THE bourbon fed his imagination, and he gave it free rein. Saw himself moving in with Carlene. Keeping his room but living with her, and the town would be fine with that, there were plenty of couples living together without being married. Cross Creek generally expected you to make it legal when there was a kid on the way, but even that was negotiable nowadays.

Still, living together that way would feel unresolved, and it wouldn't be long before he'd ask her to marry him, and even if she hadn't said anything along those lines, it would be what she was waiting to hear. He figured the wedding would be something simple, the two of them standing up in front of a town clerk or a justice of the peace, however it worked in Montana, or a minister if she wanted, because it didn't make any difference to him. Just the two of them, or maybe Andy to be his best man and a friend from the library to stand up for her, and whoever else she wanted to invite.

If there had to be something along the lines of a reception, Kalamata could cater it.

✦

HE went to refill his glass, found the bottle was empty. He must have poured a time or two without paying any real attention to what he was doing. He'd had what, eight or nine ounces of bourbon?

Didn't feel any different. Still comfortably tired, the way he always was at the end of a long day's work. Still feeling the lingering sadness that had come upon him during their lovemaking the night before; he'd gone to sleep with it and awakened with it, and it was still there.

Once they were married, they could sell her house. They'd buy something larger and more conveniently located, maybe one of the big old homes a half-mile or so east of the diner. If her house was a little snug for two people, those Victorians had far more space than the two of them needed. There'd be rooms they had no use for, rooms they'd have to furnish or leave empty.

A big kitchen, most likely. A formal dining room.

Maybe a sun parlor. A front porch, and possibly an upstairs porch as well.

Trees. A front lawn, a back yard.

Way more than either of them needed. Still, he'd always wanted a house like that. Couldn't say why, hadn't lived in anything that grand as a kid growing up. Never knew anybody in a house like that, not really.

Liked the way they looked, though. Just half a mile down Main, meant he could still walk home from the diner. Make himself a drink, take it out on the front porch. Sit in a rocker, sip his bourbon.

Two rockers, and she'd sit in the other one. The two of them, side by side, on their porch. He'd talk a little, about his day, and she'd do the same, and then they'd fall silent and just sit there, not needing to say anything, content to share the silence.

All a man could want. All he'd ever wanted, just waiting for him to say yes to it.

Outside it had resumed snowing. It wasn't working very hard at it. The big flakes were pretty as they fell through beams of light.

He sat there, watching, thinking. He looked at the empty glass, at the empty bottle.

He got to his feet.

⁓⁄⁄⁍⁝⁝⁝

BY the time he'd crossed from the doorway to the bar, the Stockman's bartender had an unopened fifth of Dant in a paper bag. When he shook his head, the fellow said, "Back to Old Crow?"

"No, Dant's good, but I don't need a bottle. Just a drink."

"Neat?"

"With water back. And make it a double."

He picked up the glass and looked at it, then looked around the room. Football on the TV with the sound off, six or seven men in the room besides himself and the bartender. Familiar faces, most of them, but nobody he'd ever spoken to, no one he knew by name.

The drink was gone, the bartender was pouring him another, helping himself to the price of it from the change on the bar top.

The water glass was still full.

He drank the second double. He'd barely been aware of drinking the first one, but now he paid attention, took a moment to tune in to the alcohol in his system. But he couldn't feel it. He knew he'd had a lot to drink, could have come up with a total, but he didn't seem to be able to feel any of it. Not that he felt sober, but he didn't really feel drunk, either. All he felt was—what?

Couldn't find the word for it.

A commercial on the TV, someone pouring beer into a glass. The last beer he'd had was when Carlene cooked that Flemish pot roast, and the last beer before that was too long ago to remember. Nothing wrong with beer, but what was the point of it? If a man was going to drink, why drink anything but whiskey?

"Another?"

Why not?

UNDER *the weather.* That had been his excuse to Carlene, breaking their date. Outside, his fingers just the least bit clumsy with the buttons of his wool Walmart jacket, he told himself that there was plenty of weather to be under. Snow still falling, with a little wind blowing up to drive it.

He'd finished his third drink and said no to a fourth, and he stood in the snow and wondered which way to go. Turn right and walk back to Mrs. Minnick's. Turn left and then what?

Walk a block and a half, he thought, to Panama Red's. He'd never been there, but he knew it by reputation. What he'd heard, they got a rougher crowd.

Standing there, trying to decide. Turn left or turn right.

That was the last thing he remembered.

WHEN his eyes snapped open he willed them shut before they had time to register an image. He tried to will consciousness away, but that didn't work. He was awake, like it or not.

And he was sprawled on the floor, one arm pinned awkwardly beneath him. He tried to learn what he could without opening his eyes, using his other senses in turn. He felt cold, and he felt pain mixed with numbness in one hand, its circulation cut off by his body weight. He smelled vomit, and he tasted blood in the back of his throat.

He heard nothing.

He didn't want to open his eyes for fear of what he'd see. But he was even more afraid to remain unknowing.

When he forced his eyes open he saw where he was, sprawled on his own floor. He moved slowly, got to his knees and then to his feet, swaying slightly as he breathed deeply and tried to get his balance.

He'd evidently made it back to his room, closed the door once he was inside. He'd sat on his chair, or tried to, and had managed to knock it over and break one of its legs on the way down.

He'd vomited. There was vomit on the rug, streaks of vomit on the front of the wool jacket. He was still wearing the jacket, but he'd managed to unbutton it before he sat down and passed out. Or he'd never gotten around to buttoning it when he headed for home.

No point trying to work it out now. No time to waste.

There was, thank God, nobody in the hallway. He went to the bathroom, cleaned himself up as well as he could. Washed his hands, his face. He'd bloodied his nose, or someone had bloodied it for him, and it hurt when he dabbed at it, but he didn't let the pain stop him. He dampened a towel and scrubbed at the stains on his jacket, and on the shirt beneath it.

Not too much blood on the jacket. More on the shirt beneath it, a long-sleeved polo shirt that had come with him from Galbraith. He didn't bother trying to clean it up, because there were other shirts he could wear, but in this weather he'd need the jacket.

Hurry up. Don't stop to think, no time to think. Later, later he could think all he wanted. More than he wanted, really.

Back to the room. Strip off the bloody shirt, toss it in the trash basket. Pull open drawers, prop his suitcase on the bed, stuff things into it. Take this, leave that, decisions made more by reflex than by thought. No time to waste, Jesus, no time to waste.

Take his drinking glass? Oh, Jesus, what did he need with that?

But he took it. And he retrieved the bloody shirt, found a plastic grocery sack to hold it, stuffed it in his bag.

THE first bus was headed for Fargo, and that wasn't the direction he wanted to go. He made himself stay in the station, perched on a stool at the lunch counter. A lifetime ago Andy had assured him he'd be taking his life in his hands if he ate there, but the thought of eating anything anywhere was impossible. He sat with a cup of black coffee. It had started out weak and sat on the heating element until it had turned to sludge, and he drank it anyway and had a second cup.

He couldn't keep from watching the door, bracing himself every time it opened, waiting for someone to walk in with a badge. At one point a pair of uniformed deputies did come in, stepped to the counter and picked up a couple of coffees to go. They both ordered it with a lot of cream and sugar, and he wondered if that would help.

He'd finished a little less than half of his own second cup when his bus came, bound for Spokane.

He relaxed, but only a little, when the bus pulled out. If Cross Creek had a *Resume Speed* sign at the edge of town, he missed seeing it. It was snowing again, so it was easy to miss things.

Minnie Pearl's home town. Funny how a line like that would stay with you.

He closed his eyes, surprised himself by dozing off.

WHEN he woke up they were still in Montana. He looked out the window and watched a freight train a few hundred yards north of the highway, running west at about the same speed as the bus. He found himself counting the cars, and he drifted off like that, and the next time his eyes opened they were in Idaho, coming into Coeur d'Alene. He didn't know how much difference it made, crossing from one state to another. It worked like a charm for Bonnie and Clyde, the boxy cop cars had to turn around and go home when they hit the state line, but things had changed some since then.

They stopped for fifteen minutes in Coeur d'Alene, with some passengers hopping off for a smoke break. He stayed where he was, and the bus pulled out on schedule, with half an hour to go before they were due in Spokane.

He'd never been to Spokane. Bigger city than he was used to, and that might make it easier to get lost in. Other hand, it was the right time of year to be heading someplace warm. Get off in Spokane, catch something southbound. There'd be towns all the way to the Mexican border, and they'd all have restaurants, and there was always a restaurant that needed somebody who knew his way around a grill.

Once he landed somewhere, he'd have to take that bloodstained shirt and lose it. He was pretty sure it was his own blood and nobody else's, because he'd evidently taken a pretty good punch in the nose, but his knuckles were bruised, so he'd very likely gotten in a few licks of his own.

Two drunks punch each other out in a barroom brawl, well, that was no way to get your picture on a post office wall. And if that's all it amounted to, why did he have to leave town? Why walk away from his room, his car, his job? His girlfriend?

There was every chance in the world no one was chasing him, just as no one had chased him out of Galbraith or the town before Galbraith. For Christ's sake, it was odds-on he hadn't been in a fight at all. Drunk as he was, he could have fallen down without getting a push.

Did he even make it to Panama Red's? Probably fell on his face before he got there, skinned his knuckles trying to break his fall, bloodied his nose, scrambled to his feet only to fall a couple more times on the way home, pausing to puke a time or two while he was at it. Then pulled himself together enough to get in the door and up to his room, and, well, the rest was clear enough. He couldn't remember it, but he could see a movie of it in his mind—the chair collapsing, the floor rushing up at him, the lights going out.

BY the time he got off the bus in Spokane, he knew he wanted someplace hot and dry. Some town in the desert, California or Nevada or Arizona.

Make a nice change.

Trailways and Greyhound shared the terminal in Spokane, and a sleepy-eyed man at the Greyhound window sold him a ticket to Sacramento. That wasn't where he wanted to wind up, but he could get a room there for a couple of nights, then plan his way south from there.

In the washroom, he stuffed the bloody shirt, sack and all, into a trash container. It was good to be rid of it, and he wasn't worried some janitor would rush it to the CSI crime lab.

His own blood, he was sure of it. All he'd had to do was clean himself up and he could have stayed in Cross Creek. Told Mrs. Minnick her chair just collapsed under him, said it was probably his own fault and paid to replace it. And if he'd been in a fight, if he'd made it to Panama Red's and raised a little hell there, well, when did that get to be a hanging offense? He was still good old Bill Thompson, decent respectable fellow, worked behind the counter at Andy's diner, and if once a year he got a wild hair and had himself a snootful, well, sheesh, man, it could happen to a bishop, you know?

He drank a cup of coffee, ate a dish of scrambled eggs and bacon. The coffee was so-so, and the eggs and bacon weren't as good as they'd have been if he'd cooked them himself, but at least he had an appetite and at least he was putting food in his stomach. He had a second cup of coffee and even thought about a piece of pie, but decided it would be too much of a disappointment after what he'd gotten used to.

If he'd stayed, if he'd gone ahead and bought Kalamata, he'd have had Hilda Parkhill working nights and week-ends. He'd have been selling pie as fast as she could bake it. The woman had a gift.

HE had to share a seat on the bus to Sacramento. His companion was an older man who mostly slept, and didn't snore too badly. He slept himself, and woke up thinking if he had any sense he'd change buses at the next opportunity and head back where he'd come from. Back to Cross Creek, back to the rooming house and the diner. Back to Carlene.

Except he couldn't.

Because he'd had to leave, and somewhere within himself he must have known that, or why break the date with Carlene? Why empty the bottle and go out for more?

Coming to, lying on the floor in a mess of blood and vomit, along with all the fear and all the dread and all the guilt, along with everything, there'd been another terrible thought.

Now's your chance. You can cut and run, you can leave it all behind.

Beside him, the old man shifted in his sleep, let out a sigh.

He let out a sigh of his own, thought again of how he'd been lying there in a pile of blood and puke.

Damned lucky he'd landed face down. You vomit while you're passed out, you could breathe it in, choke on it. Die without ever knowing what was happening.

And wouldn't that be a hell of a thing.